ONCE I WAS A BEAR

IRENE LUXBACHER

SCHOLASTIC PRESS   NEW YORK

Once I lived in
a forest of tall trees.

I splashed in cool, rushing rivers
and climbed mighty mountains.
Tumbling round and thumping down.
Always landing in the perfect place.

Mmmm . . . sweet.

My whole world fluttered and
hopped and skipped and soared.

Rest and play, day after day.
A bright circle in the sky led the way
as I roamed from one adventure
to another.

I was never
afraid.

But then, my nose smelled change in the air,
and a cold feeling swirled around me.

Time to curl up
in my earthy den
and dream . . .

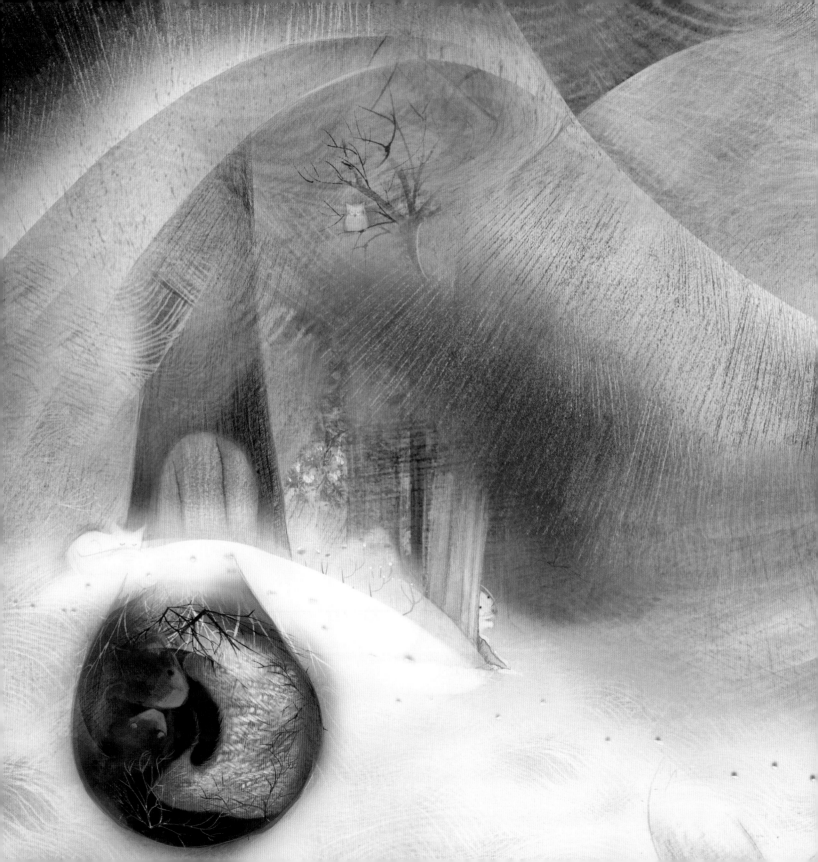

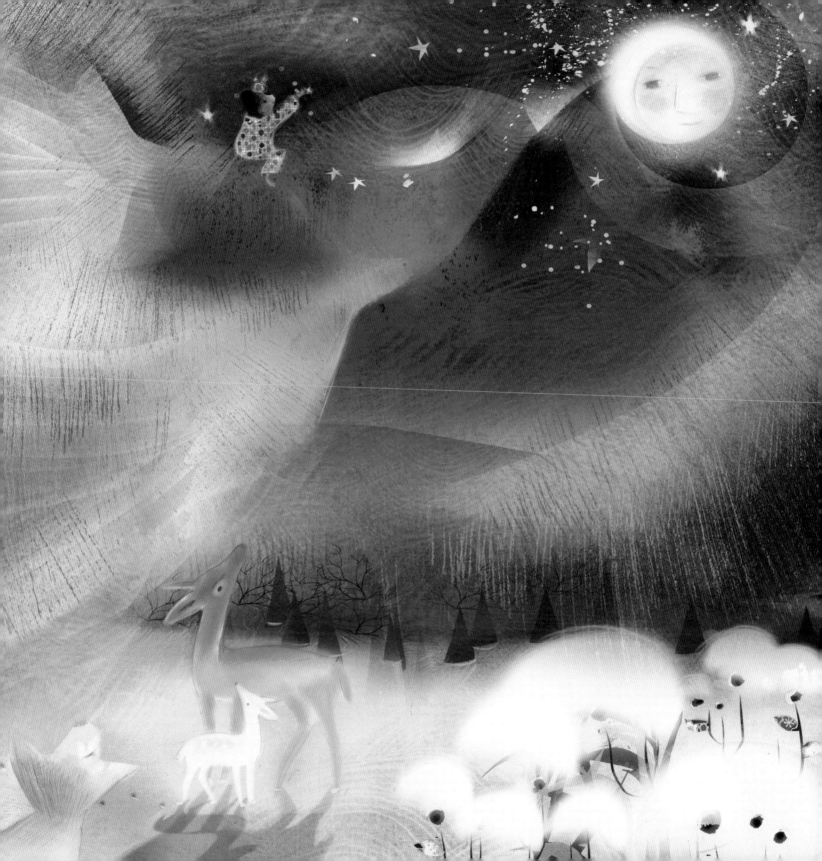

. . . I woke up in a different kind of wilderness.

Splashing and rambling,
tumbling and thumping
would have to wait.

I gulped down my berries
in a hurry.

Butterflies fluttered
in my stomach.

In this new world,
tall towers replaced
tall trees.

Loud sounds — ringing, shouting, honking! — roared around me.

Creatures stopped and stared.
I was afraid.

A new circle told me
when it was time
to rest and play
while my mind wandered.

Would others ever understand me?

Because I would never
forget that I came
from a forest of tall trees . . .

. . . and I swam in cool,
rushing rivers and climbed
mighty mountains.

But maybe
I wasn't alone.

I felt ready
to shed my fur . . .

. . . and jump and hop
and skip and soar
on a new adventure.

After all . . .

. . . once I was a bear.

FOR MY LUCA AND OUR FRIEND MAGGIE
WITH MUCH LOVE. — I.L.

ISBN 978-1-338-35633-5 • 10 9 8 7 6 5 4 3 2 1   20 21 22 23 24 • Printed in China   38 • First edition, September 2020 • Irene Luxbacher's illustrations were created with acrylic, watercolor, gouache paints, soft pencils, ink pen, and found papers, and then layered digitally. • The text type was set in Futura Bold. • The display type was set in HUGS Regular. • The book was printed on 130gsm Lumisilk matt art paper and bound at Tien Wah Press. • Production was overseen by Catherine Weening. • Manufacturing was supervised by Shannon Rice. The book was art directed and designed by Marijka Kostiw, and edited by Tracy Mack.